LINCOLNSHIRE COUNTY COUNCIL
EDUCATION AND CULTURAL SERVICES.
**This book should be returned on or before
the last date shown below.**

Yes
MOI

YOUNG
PEOPLES
SERVICE

7 DEC 2006

D1331196

THIS WALKER BOOK BELONGS TO:

_____

_____

_____

_____

JN 03396207

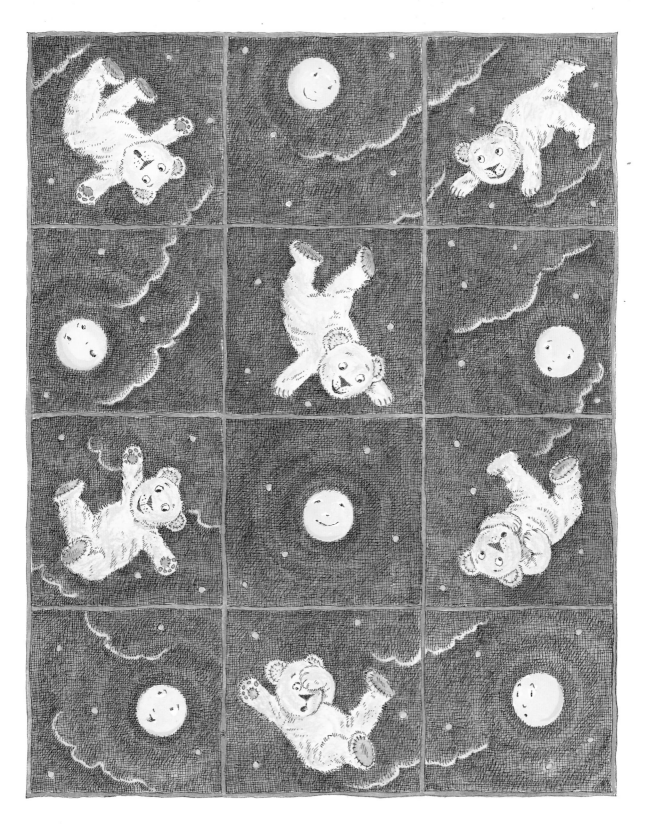

For Amelia
with our love.
S.H. & H.C.

LINCOLNSHIRE
COUNTY COUNCIL

First published 1991 by Walker Books Ltd
87 Vauxhall Walk, London SE11 5HJ

This edition published 1994

10 9

Text © 1991 Sarah Hayes
Illustrations © 1991 Helen Craig

This book has been typeset in Bembo.

Printed in Hong Kong

British Library Cataloguing in Publication Data
A catalogue record for this book is
available from the British Library.

ISBN 0-7445-3147-0

THIS IS THE
BEAR
AND THE
SCARY NIGHT

WRITTEN BY
Sarah Hayes

ILLUSTRATED BY
Helen Craig

WALKER BOOKS
AND SUBSIDIARIES
LONDON • BOSTON • SYDNEY

This is the boy
who forgot his bear

and left him behind
in the park on a chair.

This is the bear
who looked at the moon

and hoped the boy
would come back soon.

These are the eyes
which glowed in the dark.

This is the owl
who swooped in the night
and gave the bear
a terrible fright.

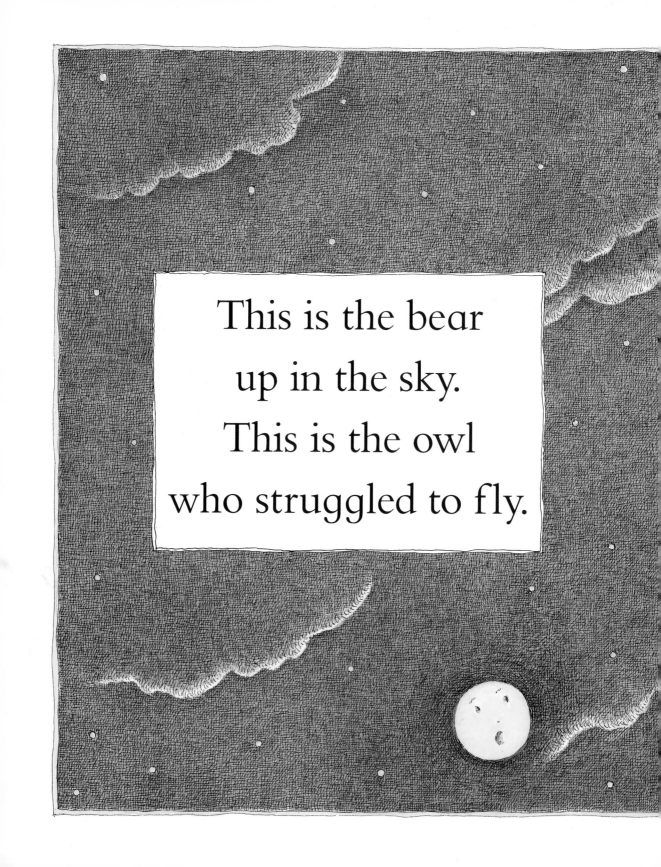

This is the bear
up in the sky.
This is the owl
who struggled to fly.

Oh no!

These are the claws
which couldn't hold on.
And this is the bear
who fell ...

This is the bear
who floated all night.

This is the dark
which turned into light.

This is the man
with the slide trombone

who rescued the bear
and took him home.

This is the bear
in a warm blue sweater
who made a friend
and felt much better.

This is the boy
who remembered his bear

and ran to the park
and found him there.

This is the bear
who started to tell

how he flew through the air
and how he fell …

and how he floated
and how he was saved
and how he was
terribly terribly brave.
And this is the boy
who grinned and said,
"I know a bear
who is ready for bed."

MORE WALKER PAPERBACKS
For You to Enjoy
Also by Sarah Hayes and Helen Craig

THIS IS THE BEAR
THIS IS THE BEAR AND THE PICNIC LUNCH
THIS IS THE BEAR AND THE BAD LITTLE GIRL

Three more great stories about the boy, the dog and the bear.

"Anyone old enough to be attached to a teddy bear will be enchanted…
Sarah Hayes' rhyming couplets work very well, and Helen Craig's
illustrations are just right." *Wendy Cope, The Daily Telegraph*

This Is the Bear   0-7445-0969-6
This Is the Bear and the Picnic Lunch   0-7445-1304-9
This Is the Bear and the Bad Little Girl   0-7445-4771-7

£4.99 each

MARY MARY

A contrary girl meets and sorts out a ramshackle giant.

"Helen Craig's pictures of the giant are just right." *The Teacher*

0-7445-2062-2   £4.99

CRUMBLING CASTLE

Three stories about the wizard Zebulum, his crow assistant
Jason, and their weird and wonderful friends.

"Gentle, cosy magic for solo readers at the lower end of the
junior school who will enjoy Helen Craig's amusing, detailed
line drawings." *Books for Keeps*

0-7445-6082-9   £3.50

Walker Paperbacks are available from most booksellers, or by post from B.B.C.S., P.O. Box 941, Hull, North Humberside HU1 3YQ

24 hour telephone credit card line 01482 224626

To order, send: Title, author, ISBN number and price for each book ordered, your full name and address,
cheque or postal order payable to BBCS for the total amount and allow the following for postage and packing:
UK and BFPO: £1.00 for the first book, and 50p for each additional book to a maximum of £3.50.
Overseas and Eire: £2.00 for the first book, £1.00 for the second and 50p for each additional book.

Prices and availability are subject to change without notice.